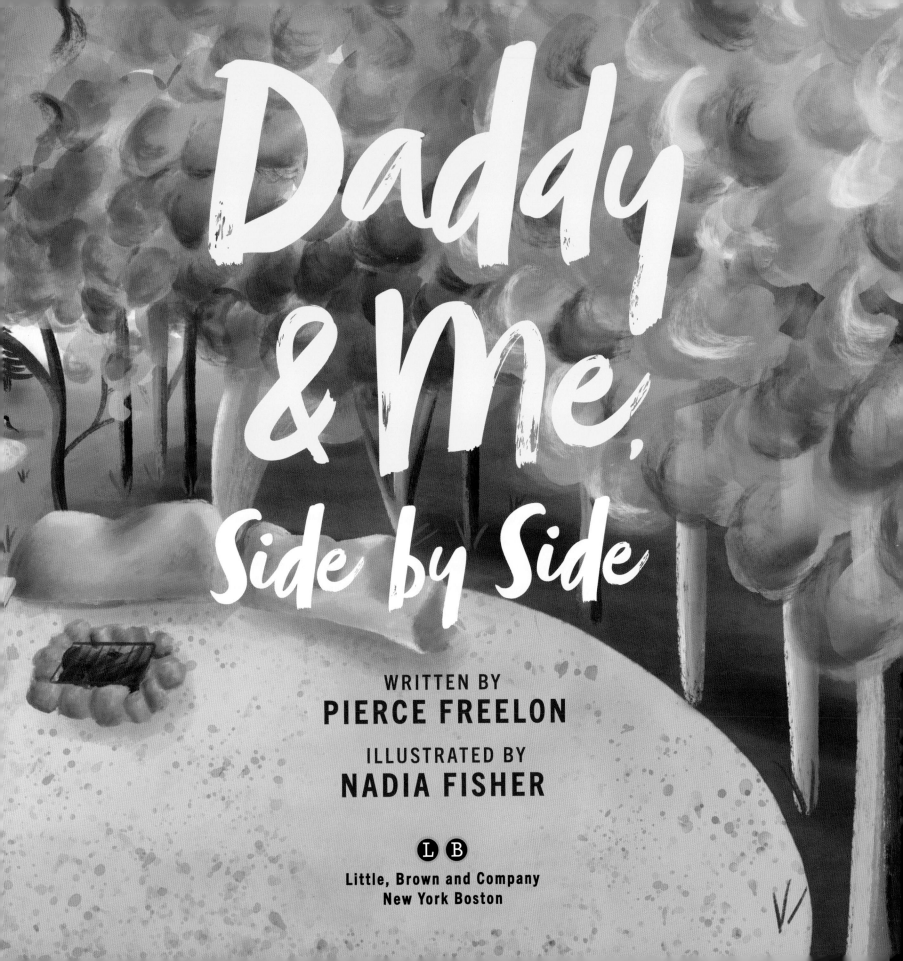

Daddy & Me, Side by Side

WRITTEN BY
PIERCE FREELON

ILLUSTRATED BY
NADIA FISHER

L B

Little, Brown and Company
New York Boston

Before the sun is in the sky I hear my daddy's rustling. "Grand rising," he says as he kisses me awake.

Unzip the tent—*brrrr!*
"Is morning always this cold out here?" I ask.
Daddy shakes his head, says we'll feel warmer
once we're moving.

The leaves on the ground
crunch under our feet
as we pack our fishing rods
and start our adventure,
side by side.

"I had fun here when I was your age.
Your pop-pop and me. It was our special place.
Feels like so long ago, feels like yesterday."

Together Daddy and Pop-Pop crossed creeks, jumping from rock to rock.

They listened to the frogs' songs as they hopped over logs.

Pop-Pop patched up his scrapes
and kissed his tears.

Now it's our turn. Together we trek
through trees and climb over boulders.

We listen to birdsong, and sometimes
I ride on Daddy's solid oak shoulders.

We dig for worms under the moss.

Daddy teaches me to bait just like Pop-Pop
taught him. Pierce the worm with the hook,
then cast my line.

We sit side by side as we wait
and wait
and wait
until my rod starts to shake, and we reel
in a bigmouth bass splashing from the lake.

Water sprays on Daddy's proud face and streams from his eyes like tears, leaving salty streaks on his acorn-colored cheeks.

"Just thinking about Pop-Pop and how he loved this spot on the bank here with me, sitting side by side."

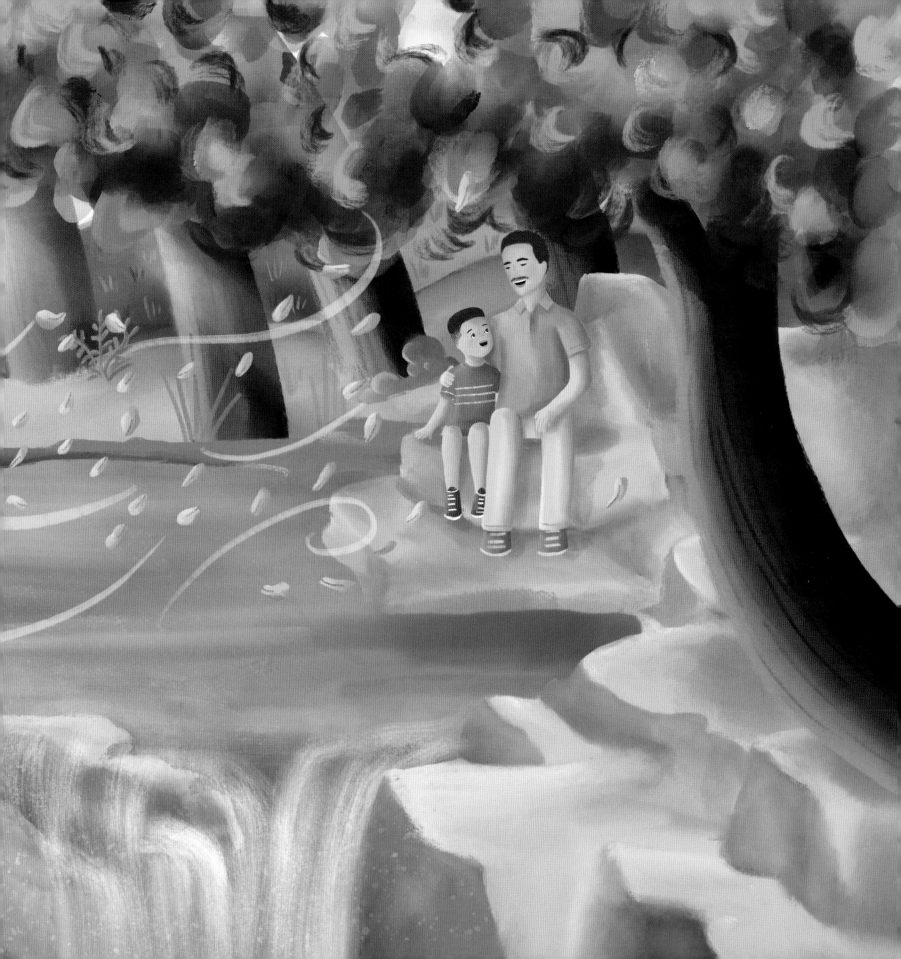

My strong daddy, I hold on to him tight, and together we remember Pop-Pop's curious mind, Pop-Pop's gentle smile.

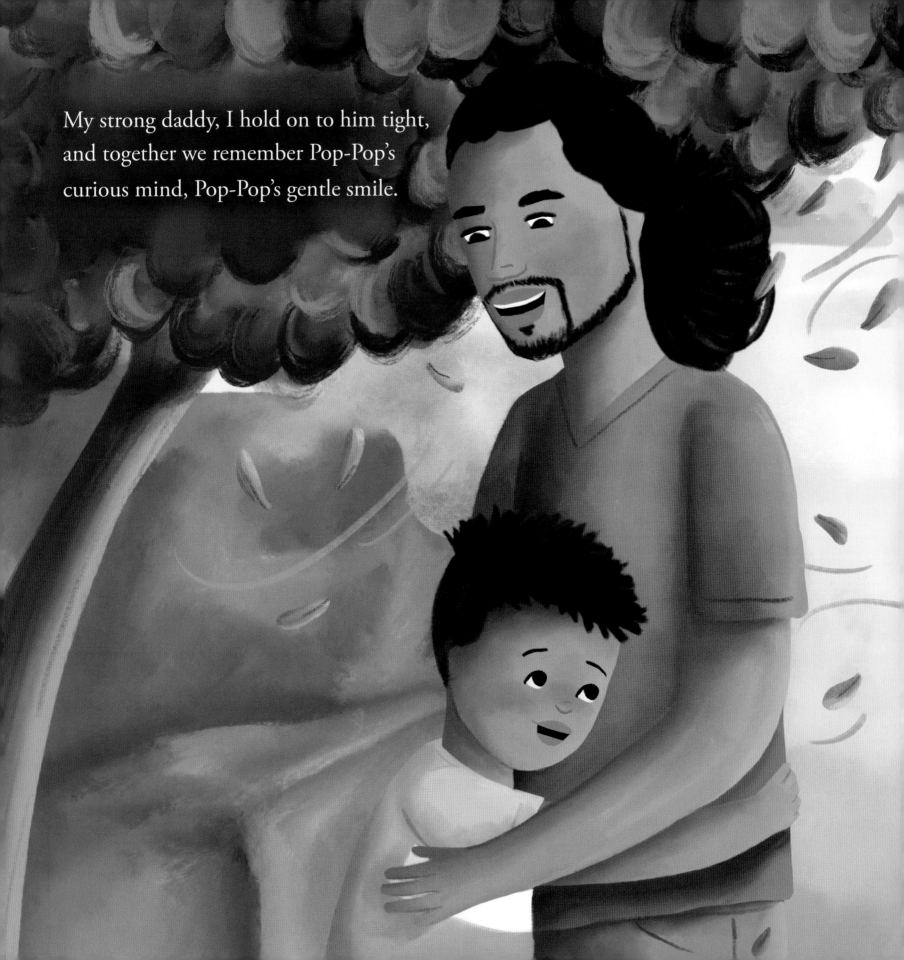

Are we looking under the
same rocks?

Weaving through the
same trails?

Resting beneath the same magnolia tree
as we sit still, listen, and breathe?

We take our catch back to camp.
Fresh fish for dinner in the evening breeze.

"I miss Pop-Pop," I whisper.

It feels safe to admit that out here in the quiet.
Daddy's eyes swell. He says, "It doesn't have to be
a secret. We feel what we feel. It's okay to let it out."

We roast marshmallows, then capture lightning bugs, and soon it's time to be zipped in my sleeping bag.

The moon is in the sky, and
I dream of Pop-Pop as Daddy
and I sleep side by side.

FOR JUSTICE, ANDRE, AND DAD, MY BELOVED ADVENTURERS —PF

TO MY FAMILY, INCLUDING THOSE WHO CAME BEFORE ME —NF